THAT DOG!

Weekly Reader Books presents

THAT DOG!

by Nanette Newman
pictures by
Marylin Hafner

Thomas Y. Crowell
New York

THAT DOG!

Text copyright © 1980, 1983 by Bryan Forbes Ltd.
Illustrations copyright © 1983 by Marylin Hafner
All rights reserved. No part of this book may be
used or reproduced in any manner whatsoever without
written permission except in the case of brief quotations
embodied in critical articles and reviews. Printed in
the United States of America. For information address
Thomas Y. Crowell Junior Books, 10 East 53rd Street,
New York, N.Y. 10022. Published simultaneously in
Canada by Fitzhenry & Whiteside Limited, Toronto.
1 2 3 4 5 6 7 8 9 10
First American Edition

Library of Congress Cataloging in Publication Data
Newman, Nanette.
    That dog!

    Summary: After Barnum dies, Ben is sure he'll never
want another dog, but a stray he finds on the way home
from school changes his mind.
    [1. Dogs—Fiction]   I. Hafner, Marylin, ill.   II. Title.
PZ7.N4853Th 1983   [Fic]   81-43892
ISBN 0-690-04229-9   AACR2
ISBN 0-690-04230-2 (lib. bdg.)

for

Ros, Graham, and Barney
—N.N.

Olivia Brown
—M.H.

"That dog's barking again," said Mrs. Higgs crossly, looking over the fence that separated the two gardens.

"He's not," said Ben. "He's talking."

"Sounds like barking to me," said Mrs. Higgs.

"It would," said Ben. "Come on, Barnum," he called. "Come and help me with my homework."

"Ridiculous," snorted Mrs. Higgs.

Some mornings Mrs. Higgs would be getting the milk off the doorstep when Barnum and Ben were leaving.

"He's snarling," she'd say.

"He's smiling," said Ben. "He's just happy."

"Huh!" said Mrs. Higgs, who never looked happy, ever.

Ben and Barnum had been together for as long as Ben could remember.

They had grown up together and Ben had taught Barnum everything he knew.

"He can't do anything," said Mrs. Higgs.

"He can do tricks," said Ben.

"What sort of tricks?" said Mrs. Higgs.

"Kill!" said Ben, and Barnum stood and put his paws on Mrs. Higgs's shoulders.

"Get him off!" screamed Mrs. Higgs. "You call that a trick?" she said, running up the path.

"Definitely," said Ben.

Barnum's favorite sport was soccer.
When Ben's team got together he was
always included. He didn't mind whether
he was goalie or center forward, or what.
He made sure they won the match against
the Markham Street team—admittedly
by hiding the ball until suppertime.

"But still," said Ben to his team afterward, "it was quick thinking."

"It was cheating," said one of the Markham Street team.

"Barnum never cheats," said Ben, and Ben's team gave Barnum a cheer, to make sure he didn't feel hurt by the remark.

One day when Ben and Barnum were shopping, Mrs. Higgs started shouting. "He's sniffing in my basket again!"

"No, Mrs. Higgs," said Ben patiently, "he was simply offering to carry it home for you."

"Really!" said Mrs. Higgs, stamping off into the drugstore.

Sometimes Barnum went to parties.
Not the organized kind, but the ones
that just happened. It would usually
be on a Sunday morning when Ben was
taking him for his favorite walk in
the park. Suddenly there would be lots
of dogs—old friends, new friends—

and off Barnum would go and have a
great time. Chasing was his favorite
game, particularly chasing little,
spoiled dogs whose owners would pick
them up, just when the game was getting
going. Barnum wasn't really a young dog
anymore, but he could still act like a puppy.

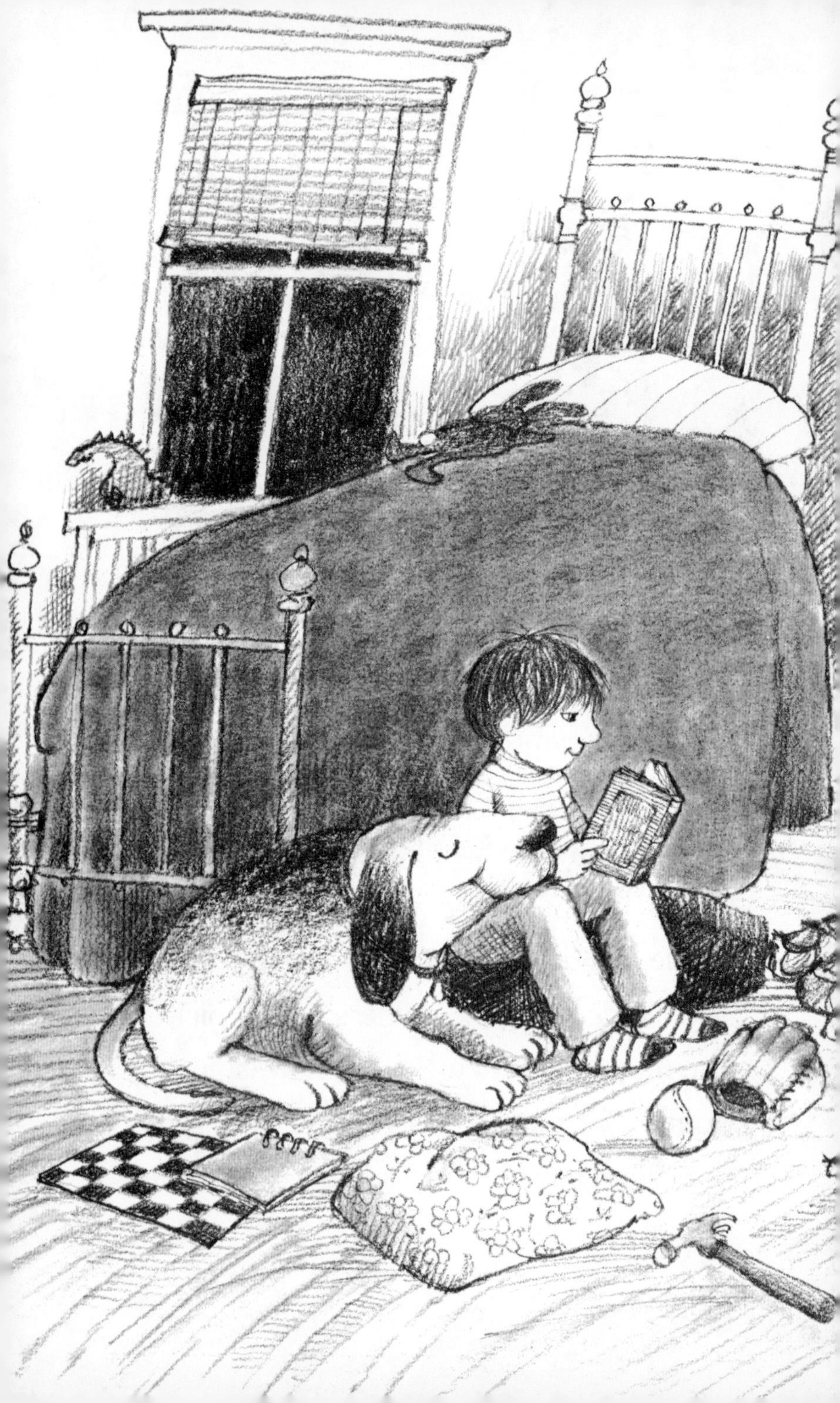

Sometimes Ben and Barnum would
spend quiet evenings together, reading.
Ben would read aloud to Barnum, and
Barnum would put his head in Ben's lap
and quietly concentrate on the story.
His favorite was *Treasure Island*.
He liked the sea songs best.

"That dog's whining," shouted Ben's
mother from downstairs.

"He's singing," said Ben.

Barnum wasn't allowed to be fed when the family was having supper. He would sit by Ben's chair and try to look sad and hungry, but Ben's mother would say: "You are not to feed him food off your plate, Ben."

"No, Mother," said Ben, with his fingers crossed under the table.

Sometimes Ben would manage to pass the juiciest piece of meat into Barnum's mouth while everybody was busy talking, and Barnum would swallow it quickly, so that no one would notice. There would just be a quick look between Ben and Barnum, then Barnum would put back on his "nobody-ever-feeds-me" look.

"That dog," said Mrs. Higgs.

"Do you mean Barnum?" said Ben.

"That dog has stolen my lamb chop."

"Never," said Ben. "Mrs. Higgs, I ask you, does Barnum look like a thief?"

Barnum sat wagging his tail and panting.

"Yes," said Mrs. Higgs.

"That woman," said Ben to Barnum as they walked down the street, "has no heart."

Barnum agreed and licked the last bit of lamb chop from around his mouth.

At night Ben and Barnum slept in the same room. When Ben's mother came in to say good night, Barnum would be lying under his blanket in the corner, yawning and stretching. The minute the door was closed he was on the bed, snuggled up to Ben. In the morning, he woke Ben by pushing his cold nose under Ben's chin and licking his ear. Ben was never once late for school.

"That dog's been digging up my garden again."

"He's trying to be helpful, Mrs. Higgs," said Ben. "I think he knew it was difficult for you to dig."

Barnum cried when Ben was scolded,

listened when Ben had a problem,
was always ready for some fun,
and loved Ben as much
as Ben loved him.

hen, one day, Barnum died.

"He was getting old," said Ben's mother, kindly.

"He wasn't," said Ben, crying.

"He had a great life," said Ben's father.

"He didn't suffer," said the veterinarian. "He'd just had a long and happy life—it was time for him to go. It happens to us all."

"But I didn't want it to happen to Barnum," said Ben.

"I know," said the vet.

The nice old man across the street
who sometimes gave Barnum a bone said:
"You know, Ben, when people get very
old they have to die to make room for
all the new people coming into the world.
It's the same with dogs."

Ben looked at him and tried not to start
crying again. He liked old Mr. Johnson.

"The other thing is, maybe God needed him," said Mr. Johnson.

"I wish God had needed Mrs. Higgs instead," said Ben.

"No," said Mr. Johnson. "She might have caused a lot of trouble up there in heaven. Barnum was a better choice."

31

Ben gave Barnum a grave with a stone
marker. Then he and Mr. Johnson said a
prayer or two, and Ben read Barnum's
favorite chapter from *Treasure Island*.
Mrs. Higgs looked over the garden fence.

"Here!" she called to Ben. She gave
Ben the best rose out of her garden to
put on Barnum's grave. She didn't have
her cross look on either.

"Thank you," said Ben.

Ben felt as if his heart had broken. He would cry at night when he put out his hand on the bed, forgetting Barnum wasn't there. He was late for school some mornings, and he didn't feel like playing soccer.

Ben's father said: "Ben, how about us getting another dog?"

"Never!" said Ben. "I never want another dog, not ever."

Old Mr. Johnson invited Ben to tea
one day. He sat in his big armchair,
with his arthritic leg up on a stool,
and they just talked about Barnum.

"Barnum would have hated for you to
be so sad. Of course you must think of
him, but have happy thoughts, not sad
ones. I want people to do that about me
when I'm gone. I hope you'll remember
that, Ben."

"I will, Mr. Johnson," said Ben.

One day when Ben was coming back from school he heard a whimper. He turned around and there was a tiny puppy.
Ben walked on, and so did the puppy.
Ben stopped, and the puppy came and sat on his foot. Ben looked at him.

"I'm lost," the puppy seemed to say.

Ben looked up and down the street. There was no one around. He picked up the puppy. There was no collar on him, and he seemed far too young to be out on his own.

"What am I to do with you?" Ben said.

The puppy had fallen asleep in his arms.

Ben took him to Mr. Johnson. They fed him and Mr. Johnson said: "Well, now, let me think. He looks like a stray to me, but we'd better make some inquiries. Would your mother let you keep him until we find him a home?"

"Well, I expect so," said Ben.

The puppy seemed to like Ben's room.
He ate a slipper and tore up a book.
He made a puddle on the floor, but when
Ben explained to him that those habits
were meant for the garden, he seemed
to understand.

41

Mr. Johnson stopped in a few days later.

"As I thought," he said, "no one's claimed him. I suppose we'll have to take him to the dog pound."

"Tomorrow," said Ben.

That night, Ben sat in his room trying
to do his French homework. The puppy
woke up and got off his foot. He looked
at Ben, trying to get him to play.

"I could never love another dog the way
I loved Barnum," said Ben.

The puppy cocked his head to one side
and seemed to listen.

"Of course," Ben said, to himself this time, "I could try and love the puppy in a different way."

"No dog could be as nice as Barnum," he said aloud.

The puppy cocked his head the other way and Ben added to himself, "But this one might be nice in a different way."

"I'd NEVER forget Barnum," he said firmly.

"But maybe I wouldn't have to," he
said to himself as he looked at the
eager puppy. "Maybe the puppy and I can
remember Barnum together."

Ben looked at the puppy a long time.
"He looks like he needs someone to love
him," Ben thought, "and I guess I need
someone to love..."

"I'll try," said Ben, and the puppy got
so excited he chewed a pencil.

"Good morning, Mrs. Higgs," said Ben.

"Oh, no! Not another one!" said
Mrs. Higgs. "And what sort of dog is
THAT, may I ask?"

"A very special sort," said Ben,
as he and Buster walked off down the
road to the park.

THE END

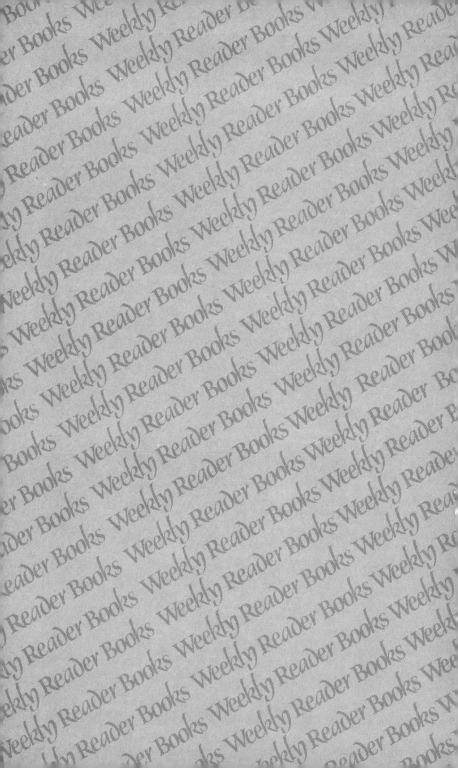